MW01107289

Sue In All Seasons

Jennifer D. Lerud

BY JENNIFER D. LERUD

ILLUSTRATED BY NADIA GORSKI

TABLE OF CONTENTS

A

SUMMER

FOR

SUE

Challenge Words

friends

sandcastles

seashells

school

wondered

A SUMMER FOR SUE

It was a perfect summer
day for playing outside.

It was not too hot. The blue sky said there would be no rain.

But Sue sat at home and looked out the window and

wondered what to do.

Sue was seven, but she did not have to go to school. School was out for the summer.

The grade school down the street stood empty and silent. No children swung on the swings or played tag in the yard.

Sue was done with her chores.

She had gotten dressed,

eaten
breakfast,

brushed
her teeth,

and made
her bed.

Her clothes and toys were
all picked up. She had even
dusted her dresser and desk.

So now Sue had nothing to do. There was no one to play with, too.

Her friends were all gone— some for all of the summer!

Meg was in China with her parents for two weeks. She was going to see giant pandas eat bamboo in a bamboo forest, see the Great Wall of China, and

see Chinese fishing boats on the water. She was going to have a lot of fun in China.

Tami was in Ohio with her grandma and grandpa all summer. They had a farm.

Tami was going to help feed the cows and chickens and ducks and geese.

She was going to play with her cousins in a treehouse. She was going to cook with her grandma and go fishing on a lake with her grandpa. Tami was going to have a lot of fun on the farm.

Lana had gone to visit her big brother. He had a house by the sea. She was going to play in the water, make castles in the sand, and find

lots of seashells. She was going to see the redwood forest, too. She was going to do lots of fun things at her big brother's house.

But Sue was not going to do any of those fun things this summer.

There were no pandas or great walls or fishing boats near her home.

There were no cows or chickens or ducks or geese. There were no treehouses. There were no seas. There was only a little pond down the road.

"Mom," Sue said as she looked out the window. "I want to do something fun."

"Do you want to play a game of checkers with me?"

asked her mom.

"Okay," Sue said. So they played checkers, but her mom won every game.

"I don't want to play checkers anymore," Sue said. "I want to do something else."

"Do you want to sail a boat on the pond?" asked her mom.

Sue liked that idea. "Yes, but we do not have a boat," she said.

"We can make one," said her mom.

So Sue and her mom made a boat out of a milk carton. They cut up the carton and painted it red. They made tiny sails out of red-striped cloth and stuck them on the boat with a wooden stick and some string.

When they were done, the boat was very pretty. Sue loved it.

"Off to the pond we go!" she said cheerfully.

Sue and her mom took the boat to the little pond down the street. It was not a very big pond, but the little milk carton boat did not need a bigger pond to float on.

Some boys were playing at the pond. They were splashing in the water and having lots of fun.

"You cannot go into the water," said Sue's mom. "The water in the pond will be too deep."

"Okay," said Sue.

They floated the boat on the water. The boys liked the milk carton boat Sue

and her mom had made. They went home to make boats of their own. Sue had fun until the boat got too soggy and started to sink.

"We can go home now," she told her mom. "The boat needs to dry out."

So Sue and her mom took the boat home.

As they went down the street, they saw a girl named Amy sitting in front of her house with a box. Something was in the box, and it was trying to get out.

"What is it, Mom?" asked Sue.

"It's a kitten," said her mom.

The kitten got out of the box, so Amy put it back in.

But the kitten kept trying to get out.

Sue and her mom stopped to see the kitten. It was a

cute little yellow ball of fur with green eyes.

"I like your kitten, Amy," said Sue. "Is it a girl or a boy?"

"It's a girl," Amy said.

"Are you giving it away?" asked Sue's mom.

"Yes," said Amy. "I have given away six kittens so far. This is the last one. When it is gone, I can go to the store with my mom for a treat."

"Do you want a kitten, Sue?" asked her mom.

"A kitten? Yes! I love kittens," said Sue.

"You will have to take good care of your kitten," said her mom. "You will have to feed it and clean it and make sure it is happy. Can you do that?"

"Yes! I can do that," said Sue.

"Amy, we will take your last kitten," said Sue's mom.

Amy gave Sue's mom the little yellow kitten, and Sue's mom gave it to Sue. "Here you go, Sue," she said. "You now have a friend to play with for the summer."

Sue was so happy! She gave the kitten a hug and

then gave her mom a hug, too. "Thank you, Mom," she said. "I love this kitten!"

Sue skipped happily home, holding the kitten in her arms.

Her mom was smiling as she watched Sue and the kitten.

"It looks like you are good friends," she said.

"We are!" said Sue.

When they got home, Sue asked her mom, "What name can I give the kitten?"

"Any name you like," said her mom.

"Okay." Sue looked at the kitten and said, "I will call you Miffy." Her mom liked that name. The kitten liked that name, too.

All day long, and for many days after, Sue played with Miffy. They played with a ball of string. They played with a little rubber mouse.

They had tea parties. Miffy liked the milk Sue gave her. She purred and purred.

They went back to the pond and sailed the red milk carton boat.

Lots of boys had milk carton boats now. There were blue boats and red boats and yellow boats and black boats. They sailed them every day at the pond. It was a lot of fun to see the boats sailing across the water.

But what Sue liked to do with Miffy the most was go

out to the backyard. There, under the shade of the big oak tree, was a pretty wooden bench. Sue sat on the bench with Miffy on her tummy and read books to her kitten.

Sue read about China's Great Wall and pandas eating bamboo. She read about farms and farm animals.

She read about fishing boats. She read about seas, seashells, sandcastles, and tall redwood trees.

Miffy loved hearing Sue read the books. She purred just as much as when she got milk at the tea parties.

As her friends came back from their trips away, they told her all about the fun they had. Sue nodded her head. She saw it all in her mind.

"What did you do this summer?" Meg, Tami, and Lana asked her.

"I did all sorts of things," Sue said. "But most of the

time, I went to faraway places."

"Where did you go?" they asked.

"Everywhere you went," she said with a smile. "And Miffy went with me. The books I read to Miffy took us there!"

Her friends were happy she had a fun summer, too.

Then they all went and sat on the bench, and Sue read them a book about kittens.

THE END

SUE'S

WALK

IN

THE FALL

Challenge Words

Halloween

mountains

pharaoh

pointed

squirrel

wait

SUE'S WALK IN THE FALL

Sue spun round and round on the swing in her backyard. It was a swing

under the big apple tree in the corner of the yard. Sue loved to swing, and today was very fun because as she swung, the leaves on the apple tree fell all around her. It was so pretty, like a fancy shower of red and gold and green!

Then Sue's mom came

outside and called her in for dinner.

"What are we going to eat?" Sue asked. If it was fish, she did not want any. She did not like fish.

"We are having beef stew," said her mother, "and homemade bread with jam and butter."

"Okay," she called back.
She hopped off the swing
and ran into the house.
She liked beef stew and
homemade bread, and now

that the nights were getting colder, that warm kind of food felt good in her tummy.

"The leaves are turning color up in the mountains," her mom said during dinner. "Maybe we should go up and take a hike."

Sue sat up tall at that idea. She loved to hike up in the mountains, even if she was seven and her legs did not go as fast as Mom's.

"Can we?" she asked.

"Sure! Let's go next Saturday," said her mother.

Sue could hardly wait for Saturday to arrive. When it finally did arrive, Sue and her mom got in the car and drove out of the city. The closer they got to the

mountains, the brighter the
colors of the leaves on the
trees became. It was like
a thousand spots of color

were fighting for someone to look at them.

"The yellow leaves are so bright and sunny," said Sue. "And the orange leaves remind me of Halloween."

"What do the red leaves remind you of?" asked her mom.

"Fire!" said Sue.

Sue could hardly sit still.

She wanted the car to stop already! When it finally did stop, she hopped out of the car, happy and eager to begin the hike. Her mom locked the car and took Sue's hand, and then they began their walk.

There was a little dirt path that went in a valley between two mountains.

Sue and her mom walked on this path. All along it were tall trees with leaves of yellow, orange, brown, and red.

It wasn't long before they saw a gray squirrel sitting on the ground. It was busy looking at something in its hands.

"What is that thing in the squirrel's hands?" Sue asked.

"That is an acorn," said Sue's mom. "Acorns come from these big oak trees. Squirrels gather acorns in the fall and hide them away to eat during the winter. Look at all of the acorns on the ground!"

Sue's mom picked up an

acorn and showed it to Sue.
It was a funny little reddish-
brown nut, smooth on the
sides and pointed on the

bottom, with a bumpy little
brown cap with a short stick
poking out on top.

"Can I keep it?" asked Sue.

"Yes," said her mom.

"The squirrel won't miss it, will he? He won't get hungry if I take it?"

"Oh, no. The squirrel has plenty of other acorns to hide for the winter."

Happy that the squirrel was going to be okay, Sue stuck the acorn in her pocket, and they began to walk again.

A little farther down the path, they came to a waterfall. It was a very tall waterfall, and Sue and her mom loved looking at the water as it bounced off one rock then another. In some spots it sprayed the sides, and lots of plants grew where it sprayed, for they liked having the water on them. Some of those plants were bright rust-red now. Fall had changed their colors, too!

"Why do the plants change colors?" asked Sue as she looked at the plants by the waterfall.

"Well," said her mom, "the plants change color because the sun isn't shining as long every day as it did in the summer. That makes the weather get colder. And when the sun doesn't shine as much and the weather gets colder, the leaves stop making food for the plant.

The green from the food in the leaves goes away and lets the other colors in the leaves take over. And that's what we see—the red or yellow that was left behind."

"Oh, I wish I were a plant so that I could turn a pretty red color like that," said Sue.

Her mom giggled. "That is a silly thing to say. You are perfect and pretty just the color you are."

They watched the waterfall for a while longer, then went farther up the path. There was a little bridge that arched across a stream. As Sue looked over the bridge and down into the water below, her mom told her the story of baby Moses and how his mother had made a basket out of rushes—almost like the tall, thick grasses around the riverbank that they were looking at—and how she had put the baby Moses inside the basket and sent him downriver to save his life.

"What happened to him?" Sue asked, scared for little baby Moses.

"He was taken out of the water by the daughter of

the king, called a pharaoh, and he became a prince under the pharaoh. Then, later on, God helped him free his people who had been made slaves by the pharaoh."

"Oh, I am so glad," Sue said, her eyes shining. She liked hearing stories about

God and about people who freed other people.

Sue took her mom's hand again, and they walked farther down the path. All of a sudden, Sue's mom stopped and went, "Shh!" She bent down and pointed so that Sue could see the two deer that her mom had seen.

The deer were standing side by side between two oak trees. Their big brown eyes watched Sue and her mom carefully. Their mouths moved as they chewed on some twigs and leaves. Then, all of a sudden, they started running away. Soon they were leaping between the trees, nothing but a brown blur with a spot of white sticking up in the air. And then they were gone.

"Deer are pretty," said Sue.

"Yes, they are," agreed her mom. "It is getting late. Do you want to turn around and run fast like deer to the car?"

"Okay!" said Sue.

So Sue and her mom ran fast down the path like two deer. They got to the bridge and stopped to catch their breath. Later, as they ran over the bridge, Sue waved goodbye to it, thinking about the story of the baby Moses.

Sue and her mom ran like deer from the bridge down the path to the waterfall. As they stopped to catch their breath by the waterfall, Sue waved goodbye to the pretty falling water and all of the red and yellow plants that had lost their green like the tree leaves had.

Sue and her mom ran to where they had seen the squirrel. It was still there! And there was another squirrel with it, too. Both

of them had lots of acorns
stuck in their cheeks. They
looked so funny! As Sue and
her mom ran up to them,
they darted away as fast as

can be. Soon they were high up in the trees, hiding their acorns from Sue and her mom.

Sue giggled at the squirrels. They were so funny!

Soon they were in the car and driving back home. Sue watched the colorful trees as the car sped by them, faster than the two deer. The world was changing, turning colder. The plants were not making much food, and their leaves showed the change.

"I love all of the colors," said Sue to her mom. "Fall is a very pretty time of year."

"I love it, too," her mom said. "But not as much as I love you!"

THE END

A

SNOWY

DAY

FOR SUE

Challenge Words

blanketed

carpeted

cocoa

glitter

glittering

A SNOWY DAY
FOR SUE

Sue woke up to see white,

fluffy stuff sticking to her

bedroom window. "Snow!" she said. "It's snowing outside!"

She quickly hopped out of bed and looked out her frosted window.

Snow lined the trees.
Snow carpeted the grass.

Snow was heaped in
piles along the road and
blanketed the houses and
cars.

Snow even covered the
little bench in the backyard
where Sue sat in the
summer and read books to
her yellow cat, Miffy.

Sue got dressed in blue jeans and a red shirt, then went to find her mom. She was in the kitchen making pancakes for breakfast.

"Mom!" Sue said. "Are you happy it snowed last night?"

"Yes, I am," her mom said with a smile. "Do you want to play in the snow today?"

"Oh, yes!" said Sue.

"What do you want to do?"
Mom asked.

Sue had to think for a bit.
Then she said, "First, I want
to build a
snowman.
Then I
want to ice
skate on
the pond.
And then

I want to sled down Bluebird Hill!"

"That sounds like a lot of fun," said her mom. "Clean up your room after breakfast, and then you can go outside."

"Yay!" said Sue.

Sue ate two big pancakes and drank a glass of milk.

After that she washed her hands, brushed her teeth, made her bed, and cleaned up her room.

Her mom was very happy. "You washed your hands and brushed your teeth without being told! What a big girl you are!"

Sue just grinned and said, "Can I go outside now?"

"Yes. Let's get on your winter clothes so you will stay warm," said her mom.

Sue's mom helped Sue pull her pink snow pants up over her blue jeans.

Then she helped Sue zip up her pink winter coat with glittering snowflakes on it.

Next she helped Sue put on the purple hat and mittens and scarf that Grandma had made for her last year.

Last of all, her mom helped Sue put on her snow boots.

Now Sue was ready for the cold! She gave her mom a kiss and went outside to build a snowman.

Sue had built a snowman last winter with her dad. He'd started by making a snowball. Then he'd pushed the snowball across the snowy ground.

As he did, the snowball picked up more and more

snow until it was a very big snowball.

That became the snowman's big bottom. Two more big snowballs became

the snowman's middle and head.

Sticks became its arms.

Sue's dad had let her put on the snowman's coal eyes, blue hat, and carrot nose.

So Sue started to make a snowball just like her dad, but the snow did not stick together into a ball.

It just sprinkled down like glitter between her mittens.

"Oh no," she said. "This snow is no good for making a snowman."

With a sad face, Sue stomped into the house to tell her mom.

"I'm sorry the snow isn't good for building a snowman," her mom said. "Let's go to the pond and see if the ice is good for ice skating." So Sue's mom put on her winter coat, hat, and boots. Then she got Sue's ice skates, and they walked down the road to the pond.

It was not a very big pond, but the water was pretty deep in the middle. In the summer, the water almost came up to Sue's neck.

But she was not very tall yet. She was still growing.

Bobby Jones was at the pond. He was nine.

He had ice skates with him, but he was not skating. He was sitting in the snow, looking sad.

"Hi, Bobby," said Sue. "Why are you sad?"

Bobby brushed a tear from his eye and sniffed. "I

wanted to skate, but the ice is too thin. Mom said I had to check it first. So I threw a heavy rock on the ice, but it

broke." He nodded to a hole in the ice and frowned.

"Your mom is very smart," said Sue's mom. "I'm glad you tested the ice and didn't fall into the cold, icy water."

Bobby gave a sad nod. "Yes, I'm glad I didn't fall in. But I wanted to go ice skating so badly! Now I have nothing to do!"

"Sue is going sledding on Bluebird Hill," said Sue's mom. "Do you want to go sledding with her?"

"That sounds like fun," he said.

"Hey, Mom," Sue said, tugging her mom's coat sleeve, "when we're done sledding, can Bobby come to our house for some hot cocoa and cookies?"

"If his mom says it's okay," said Sue's mom.

Bobby hopped to his feet. A big grin lit his face. "I'll go ask my mom and be back as fast as I can!"

Bobby ran home with his ice skates. When he came running back again, his skates were gone, and now he was carrying a shiny red sled.

"Mom says I can go sledding with you!" Bobby said, grinning. "And I can have hot cocoa and cookies, too!"

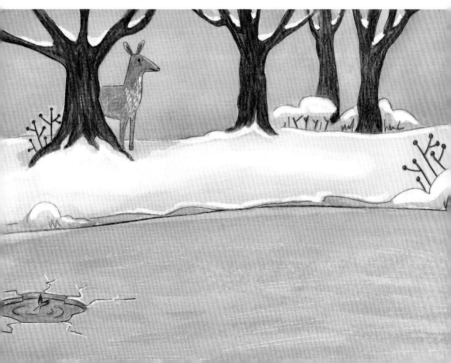

"Yay!" said Sue and her mom.

Bluebird Hill was a small hill, just perfect for

sledding. It was not too steep and not too flat. There were no rocks to crash into. There were no places where little cliffs dropped off. There were some trees and bushes where the bluebirds lived, but they were not in the way.

Sue waved to her mom as

she and Bobby walked up the snowy hill with their sleds. Up at the top, they sat down carefully and held on tight to their sleds.

"Ready—set—go!" Bobby called.

Down they went! The snow was perfect for sledding!

It felt soft and gentle under them as they slid down the hill like rockets.

"Whee!" shouted Sue.

"Yahoo!" yelled Bobby.

They reached the bottom of

the hill, then climbed back up and went down again.

Sledding was fun! But after a while, Sue and Bobby were getting tired and cold.

"Time to stop?" asked Sue's mom. She had been watching them sled to make sure they were safe.

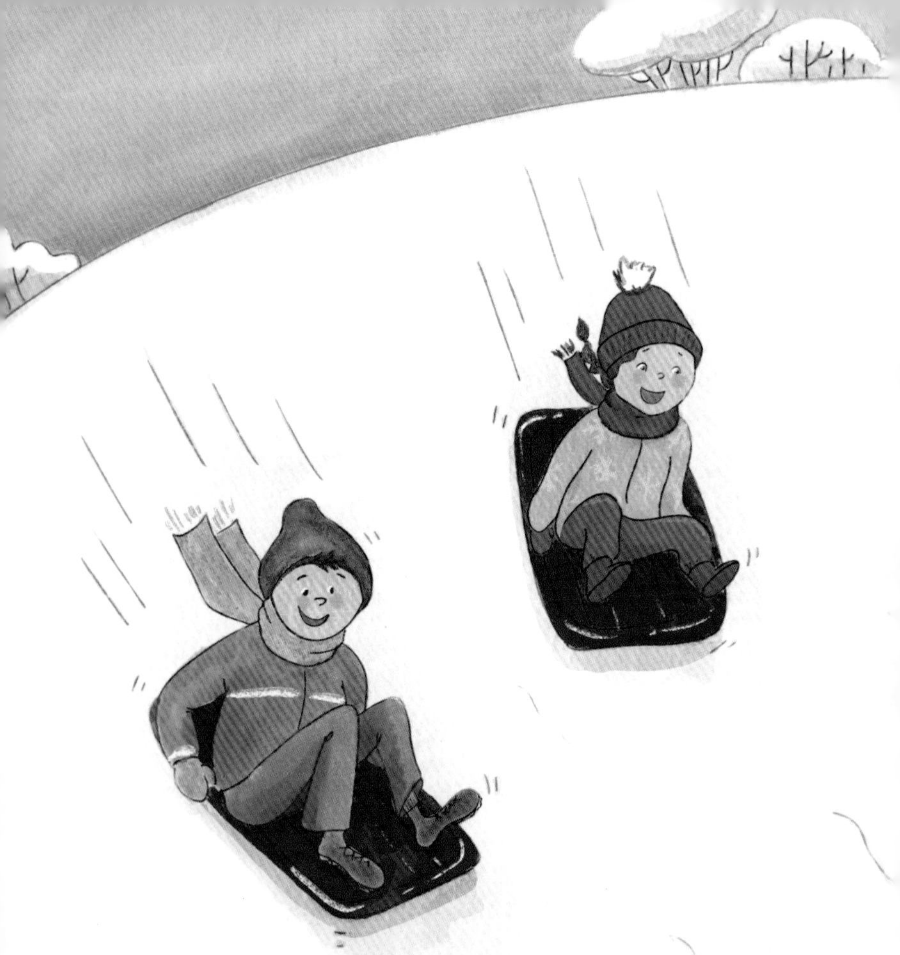

"Yes!" said Sue and Bobby together.

Their noses were cold and red. Their fingers were tingling. Their toes were like little balls of ice.

They wanted to go inside and be warm!

So they picked up their sleds and went to Sue's house.

Soon Sue and Bobby were sitting before a warm, crackling fire, eating cookies and sipping hot cocoa.

Sue's mom read a book to them as they ate. It was about a boy and a girl playing in the snow!

"That was a good story," Bobby said when it was time for him to go home. "Thank you for reading it to me. Thank you for everything. I had a lot of fun."

"You're welcome," said Sue's mom. "I'm glad you had fun."

That night as Sue was being tucked into bed, her mom asked, "What was

the best thing about your day, Sue? Was it making a snowman?"

Sue shook her head and giggled. Her mom was being funny.

"No, that wasn't it," she said.

"Was it finding Bobby at the pond?" her mom asked next.

Sue giggled and shook her head again. "No, that wasn't it."

"Was it going sledding with Bobby and having treats and a story?"

Sue gave a big smile. That had been lots of fun. But

that had not been the best thing about her day. So she said, "No, that wasn't it."

"Then what was the best thing?" asked her mom.

Sue grinned and said, "It was you, Mom."

"It was me?"

"Yes, it was you."

"Why was it me?" asked Sue's mom.

"Because you were happy there was snow outside, instead of being sad. And you were proud of me when I washed my hands and brushed my teeth without being asked.

"And because you helped me get on my snow clothes.

And because you made
Bobby feel smart when he
was sad that the ice was too

thin. And because you let him go sledding with me, and you gave us cookies

and hot cocoa and read us a story by the fire.

   "Oh, Mom, you made me

and Bobby so happy today! That's why you were the best thing!"

"Oh, thank you. I love you, Sue," said her mom. She gave Sue a hug and a kiss.

"I love you, too, Mom," Sue said. "And I want to be just like you when I grow up."

"Oh, you are a sweet one!"

said her mom.

After her mom finished tucking her in and left the room, Sue looked up at her bedroom window. The white, fluffy snow from this morning was gone. It had gotten warmer during the afternoon. Most of the snow had melted. So Sue gave a little sigh and said, "I hope it snows again tonight, so I can have a day like today all over again!"

THE END

SPRING

FLOWERS

FOR

SUE

Challenge Words

apricot

crocuses

daffodils

dandelions

Saturday

teacher

SPRING FLOWERS
FOR SUE

"Your birthday is next Saturday, Sue," said Sue's

mom. "What do you want for a gift?"

Sue was eating breakfast. She held her spoon in the air, thinking about what she wanted.

"Flowers," she finally said.

"Flowers?" Her mom looked surprised. "What kind of flowers?"

"The kind that grow outside," said Sue.

It was spring, and sometimes on her birthday there were flowers growing in the flower beds around her home. But sometimes on her birthday the ground was cold, still covered with snow. This year snow was still on the ground. But some of the flowers in the flower beds had green leaves poking up out of the ground already. And today was Sunday, so there was almost a week before her birthday on Saturday.

Sue's mom did not look hopeful. "I don't think we will have flowers for your birthday this year," she said. "It is going to be cold all week. Is there anything else you want for your birthday?"

Sue asked for a birthday outfit, but what she wanted most was the flowers. Sue loved flowers. She had missed them all winter long. She loved their little petals, so colorful and pretty. They made her feel happy inside, and they smelled *so* good!

At church, Sue drew pretty

flowers during coloring time. Her teacher said they were very pretty. Sue told her teacher that she wanted flowers for her birthday on Saturday. Her teacher frowned, just a little, and then smiled. "It will be a nice birthday present if you get your wish," she said.

"We will pray that you get flowers for your birthday. It is spring, and flowers come in the spring. So maybe your prayer will be answered." But the Sunday school teacher looked out the window and frowned just a little again. Then the Sunday school class prayed

that Sue would have flowers
for her birthday.

On Monday, it snowed. Sue
looked out her bedroom
window and said, "Stop
snowing! How are the

flowers going to grow if you keep snowing?"

The snow kept falling all day long. Sue watched it out the window as she drew more flowers.

"Those are nice flowers you are drawing," said her mom before dinner.

"Thank you," said Sue as she picked up her drawings so her mom could set the table. "I hope I have flowers like these on my birthday."

Her mom looked out the window and frowned.

On Tuesday, Sue woke up to find the snow melting. "Yay!" she said with a smile. But by noon it got cold again—too cold for the snow to melt. "Oh, boo!" she said with a frown. After lunch, Sue drew lots and lots of flowers.

On Wednesday, Sue and her mom went to the store

to get Sue a new birthday outfit. Sue put on lots of pretty clothes and finally

found an outfit she liked—
blue pants and a blue shirt.
On the shirt were three
little orange kittens playing
with some yellow yarn.

Sue liked her new
birthday outfit, but she
still wanted flowers. So she
drew more flowers when
they got home.

That night before bed, Sue
prayed again for the snow
to go away. She prayed for it
to get warm so there would

be flowers for her birthday.

Her mom smiled as she tucked Sue into bed. "I hope you get your birthday flowers," she said. "God gives us the snow to help water the flowers and plants to make them grow. But maybe God wants it to stay cold for a while, Sue.

We will have to let Him choose what to do."

Sue nodded and snuggled into her bed, but she hoped

God wanted her to have her
birthday flowers.

On Thursday morning
Sue woke up to find the sun

shining. Water was dripping off the roof in front of her bedroom window. It was a warm day! Sue smiled. She hopped out of bed, brushed her teeth, got dressed, and went down the stairs to the kitchen. Her mom was making breakfast.

"It's warm today!" said Sue.

"Yes, it is," agreed her mom. "The snow is melting."

Water dripped from the house and onto Sue's head

as she went outside after breakfast. The snow was melting, but it still covered the flower beds.

"Maybe the snow will be gone for my birthday," said Sue. Then, as she went inside to draw more flowers again, she added, "Please, snow, go away!"

Friday came. Friday was the day before Sue's birthday. Friday was another warm day, and that made Sue very happy. The snow was melting, and the green leaves of the flowers in the garden were growing taller and getting bigger.

Sue went to bed feeling very happy. She was more hopeful now than she had been before.

The next morning, Sue

woke to see the sun shining in her window.

"It's my birthday today!" said Sue. It was Saturday, the day she turned eight years old.

She hopped out of bed and skipped to her bedroom window to see what it looked like outside. Her eyes sparkled, and a smile lit her mouth when she saw her backyard.

The apple tree in the backyard had fluffy white blossoms on it. It looked so pretty, all white like a snowball made of flowers. It made Sue want to sing, so she sang the song "Popcorn Popping on the Apricot Tree."

Sue's mom had said that apples grew from those white blossoms, not popcorn or apricots. And it took a long time for apples to grow big and be ready to eat. But, for now, she liked to think that it was a popcorn tree!

She looked to see what other things were growing in the backyard.

But below the oak tree in the backyard, in her mom's flower garden near a little wooden bench, were some of the green leaves that had poked up out of the ground before. Her mom said they were crocuses—and now they were more than just leaves. There were purple crocus flowers, too!

"Crocus flowers for my birthday!" said a happy Sue. She jumped out of bed and got dressed in her new

birthday pants and shirt. Then she put on her socks and shoes and went clomp, clomp, clomp down the stairs to the kitchen to go outside. She wanted to see those flowers!

Sue's mom was in the kitchen making breakfast.

"Happy birthday, Sue," she said, a grin on her face.

"Did you see? You got your birthday flowers!"

"I did!" Sue said. "I am so happy! I am going outside to see them."

And off Sue went to see the flowers. There were apple blossoms and crocuses and a few yellow daffodils. There were dandelions (Mom didn't like that!) and some pretty little white snowdrops dangling on their tender stems.

Sue ran back into the house, and then she saw what her

mom had done there!

All around the kitchen walls were the flowers she had been drawing all week. The kitchen was full of flowers, too!

"Oh, Mom! I love you,"
Sue said. "And I love God
for answering my prayers.
And I love all of my birthday
flowers!"

THE END